THE
UGLY
DUCKLING

THE
UGLY DUCKLING

A TALE FROM HANS CHRISTIAN ANDERSEN
RETOLD AND ILLUSTRATED BY
LORINDA BRYAN CAULEY

HARCOURT BRACE JOVANOVICH, PUBLISHERS
SAN DIEGO   NEW YORK   LONDON

Other Books Illustrated by
Lorinda Bryan Cauley

The Elephant's Child

The Goose and the Golden Coins

LIBRARY OF CONGRESS CATALOGING IN PUBLICATION DATA
Cauley, Lorinda Bryan.
The ugly duckling.
SUMMARY:
An ugly duckling spends an unhappy year
ostracized by the other animals in the barnyard
before he grows into a beautiful swan.
[1. Fairy tales] I. Andersen, Hans Christian,
1805–1875. Den grimme ælling. II. Title.
PZ8.C285Ug [Fic] 79-12340
ISBN 0-15-292435-3
ISBN 0-15-692528-1 pbk.

D E
HBJ

Gratefully, to Barbara

It was lovely out in the country in the summer. The cornfields were yellow, the oats were green, and the hay stood in stacks in the meadows. All around the fields were great forests, and in the middle of these forests lay deep lakes. In a sunny spot stood an old manor house with a deep moat around it. Great burdock leaves grew along its walls down to the water. It was under one of these leaves that a duck was sitting on her nest. Her ducklings were taking such a long time to hatch that she was beginning to lose patience. She hardly ever had a visitor because the other ducks would rather swim around the moat than sit and gossip with her.

At last one egg after another began to crack. "Piep! Piep!" cried little ducklings, poking their heads through their shells.

"Quack! Quack!" said the mother duck as they all came tumbling out.

"How big the world is!" the ducklings said, for certainly there was more room under the burdock leaf than there was inside an egg.

"You don't think *this* is all the world?" said their mother.
"It stretches all the way to the other side of the garden, right
into the parson's field. Though I have never been that far!" She
got up to see if all the eggs were hatched. The largest egg was
still there.

"Oh dear, how long is this one going to take? I'm so very
tired of sitting," she said with a sigh. And she sat down again.

Just then an old duck waddled up for a visit. "Well, how is it going?" she asked.

"There's still one egg that simply won't crack," said the mother. "But look at the others. They're the loveliest ducklings I've ever seen. They all take after their father, the wretch. He never comes to see me!"

"Let me take a look at that egg that won't crack," said the old duck. "Hmmm . . . I'll bet it's a turkey egg. I was cheated like that once. You had better get busy with your babies. As much as I quacked and snapped, it took forever to get my young ones into the water! Yes, that's a turkey egg all right. I would just ignore it and teach the other children how to swim."

"I think I will sit on it a little longer," said the mother duck. "I've sat so long now that I don't mind a few more days."

"As you please," said the old duck, and she waddled away.

At last the big egg cracked. "Piep! Piep!" said the little one as it rolled out. But it was so large and funny looking! The mother duck stared at it.

"What a big ugly duckling that is," she said. "None of the others looks like that. I wonder, could it really be a turkey chick? Well, we shall soon find out. It will go into the water even if I must kick it in myself!"

The next day was lovely. Mother Duck went down to the water with her whole family trailing behind. Splash! Into the water she jumped. "Quack! Quack!" she said as one duckling after another plunged in behind her. Under the water they sank, but came up in an instant and floated beautifully. Their legs began to work for them as they paddled about in the water. Even the large ugly duckling paddled well.

"Then, it is not a turkey," said Mother Duck. "Look how well it uses its legs and how straight it holds itself. It is indeed my child and really is quite pretty if one looks at it properly. Quack! Quack! Now come along with me and I will introduce you to the world. But mind you keep close to me and watch out for the cat!"

When they came to the duck yard, there was a terrible noise going on. Two families were fighting over an eel's head, but the cat got it after all.

"You see? That is the way of the world," said the mother duck, licking her beak and wishing she had a bite of the eel. "Step lively now and bow your necks to the old duck there. She's Spanish and the grandest of us all. Don't turn in your toes! A well-brought-up duck walks with its toes turned out, just like Mother and Father. Now bend your necks and say 'Quack!'"

And so they did. But the other ducks only looked at them with a frown and said, "Now we're going to have to put up with that mob too! As if there weren't enough of us. And look what a funny duckling that big one is!" Then one duck flew over and bit the poor ugly duckling in the neck.

"Let it alone!" cried the mother. "It won't do anyone any harm!"

"Maybe, but it's so large and peculiar looking," said the one who had bitten it. "So it's best to make it keep its place!"

"The rest of the children are pretty enough," said the old Spanish duck. "But you're right, that one is a failure. It's a pity you can't make it over again."

"Well, it may not be pretty," said the mother, "but it has a lovely disposition. And it even swims better than all of the others. I think it has just lain too long in the egg, and that's why it is not quite the right shape." She patted it on its neck and smoothed down its feathers. "Anyway, it's a drake," she said. "He will be very strong and make his way all right."

"Well, the other ducklings are charming!" said the old duck. "So make yourselves comfortable here. And if you find an eel's head, you may bring it to me."

After that they felt quite at home—except the poor ugly duckling, who was always being bitten, pushed, and jeered by the ducks and even the chickens. "He's too big and homely!" they all said. "Keep him in his place." And the turkey cock puffed himself up, got quite red in the face, and gobbled right at him. The poor duckling didn't know where to go. He was the butt of the whole duck yard.

That was how the first day went, and it got worse and worse. Even his brothers and sisters were mean to him.

They said, "We hope the cat gets you! You're an awful sight!" And the mother said, "If only you were grown and far away!" Even the girl who came to feed the poultry kicked him with her foot.

At last he ran off and flew up over the fence. The little
birds in the bushes flew up in fear.

"That is because I am so ugly!" thought the duckling and
shut his eyes. He flew on farther into the marsh, where the wild
ducks lived. Here he lay the whole night long, sad and weary.

Toward morning the wild ducks flew by and looked at their new companion. "What might you be?" they asked. The duckling turned in every direction and bowed as well as it could. "You are remarkably ugly!" said the wild ducks. "But that does not matter to us as long as you do not marry into our family."

Poor duckling! He certainly had no thoughts of marrying anyone. All he wanted was to lie among the reeds and drink a little swamp water.

He lay there two whole days, until two wild ganders came along. They had come out of their eggs only a short while before, so they were still quite lively.

"Listen, my friend," said one of them, "you're so ugly that I like you. Come and join us in another marsh. There are some sweet, lovely wild geese, all unmarried and able to say 'Quack.' You've a chance at making your fortune, homely as you are."

"Bang! Bang!" Shots resounded through the air. The two ganders fell down dead, and the water in the swamp turned red. "Bang! Bang!" came the sounds again, and a flock of wild geese rose up from the reeds. A big hunt was going on. The hunters were lying hidden all around the marsh. Blue smoke from their guns rose like clouds among the dark trees and hung across the water. The hunting dogs slashed into the mud, bending back the rushes and trampling down the reeds on every side.

The poor duckling was terribly frightened! He turned his head to hide it under his wing. But just at that moment a dreadfully big dog appeared close by. His tongue hung, dripping, far out of his mouth, and his eyes gleamed horrible and mean. He thrust his nose close against the duckling and showed his sharp teeth, then—splash!—went on without seizing him.

"Oh, heaven be thanked!" said the duckling, sighing. "I am so ugly that even the dog doesn't want to bite me!"

And so he lay quite quiet while the shots rattled through the reeds and gun after gun was fired. At last, late in the day, all became still. But the poor duckling did not dare to get up. He waited several hours before he looked around. Then he hurried from the marsh as fast as he could. He waddled over field and meadow. The wind blew so hard that he could hardly move against it.

Toward evening he came to a poor farmhouse. It was such a run-down place that it didn't know which side to fall on, so it kept on standing. The duckling huddled outside as the storm raged fiercely around him. Then he noticed that the door was off a hinge and hung so crookedly that he could slip right through the crack, which he did.

Inside lived an old woman with her cat and her hen. The cat she called Sonnie, and it could arch its back and purr. And if you stroked its fur the wrong way, it would give off sparks. The hen was called Chickabiddy Shortshanks because of her little short legs. She laid good eggs, and the woman loved her as she might her own child.

When the morning light came, they all saw the poor, strange duckling. The cat began to purr and the hen to cluck.

"What's this?" said the old woman, looking around. But since she could not see well, she thought the duckling was a grown fat duck who had lost its way. "Isn't this a rare find!" she said. "Now I shall have duck's eggs too. But first we must see if it is a drake."

And so the duckling was allowed to stay for three weeks. But no eggs came. Now the cat was the master of the household, and the hen was the lady. They were always saying, "We and the world," for they thought they were half of the world, and by far the better half. The duckling tried to explain that they were not, but the hen would not allow it.

"Can you lay eggs?" she asked.

"No."

"Then you'll please hold your tongue!"

And the cat said, "Can you curve your back and purr?"

"No."

"Then you had better not offer your opinions when sensible people are speaking."

The duckling sighed and sat in a corner. Then as fresh air and sunshine began to stream in, he had an uncontrollable urge to go for a swim on the water. He could not help telling the hen about it.

"The trouble with you is you have nothing to do. That is why you get these very strange notions. Purr or lay eggs and they will go away."

"But it is so lovely to float on the water! So refreshing to let it close over your head, and to dive to the bottom," said the duckling.

"Oh, that would be a fine amusement," said the hen, shivering. "I think you have lost your mind! Ask the cat about it. He's the cleverest one you know. Ask him if *he* likes to float on the water or dive to the bottom. Or ask our mistress, the old woman. No one is wiser than she. Do you think *she* would like to float and get water over her head?"

"You don't understand me," said the poor duckling.

"Well, if we don't understand you, I'd like to know who does! Don't be so foolish, and give thanks to your maker for all the kindness you've been given. Did you not get into a warm room in which to sleep? And do you not have company from which you can learn wise things? Just take care that you soon learn how to lay eggs or purr, or to give off sparks!"

"I think I will go out into the wide world," said the duckling.

"Yes, do go, you stupid thing!" said the hen.

And so the duckling went away. He floated on the water and dived to the bottom. But he could not make friends with any animal because of his ugliness.

Autumn came. The leaves in the forest turned yellow, red, and brown. The wind sent them dancing in the chilly air. Clouds hung heavy with hail as the raven stood on the fence, screaming with the cold.

It was enough to make one shiver just to think of it. What would the poor duckling do? Then one evening as the sun was setting in wintry splendor, a flock of birds came out of the bushes. They were dazzling white, with long, limber necks. The duckling had never seen anything so beautiful. They uttered a very strange cry. Then they spread forth their splendid wings and flew up and away to warmer lands and fair, open lakes.

As they flew high above, the duckling felt a strange
sensation as he watched them. He turned around and around in
the water and stretched out his neck toward them. Then he let
out a cry so loud and strange that it frightened even himself.
Oh, how he longed for those beautiful, happy birds! He did not
know their names or where they were flying to, but he loved
them more than he had ever loved anyone before. He would
have been glad if only they might have endured the company of
such a poor, ugly creature as he. Still he was not envious. How
could he even think of possessing such loveliness as theirs?

The winter grew cold, very cold. The duckling had to swim around in the water to keep it from freezing entirely. But every night the hole in which he swam got smaller and smaller. At last he became so exhausted that he could move no more. And he froze fast into the ice!

Early in the morning a farmer came by. When he saw what had happened, he broke the ice with his wooden shoe and carried the poor duck home to his wife.

When the duckling warmed up, he became himself again. But when the children wanted to play, the duckling feared they would hurt him. He fluttered in his terror up into the milk pan, and milk spurted all over the room. The woman screamed and slapped her hands, at which the duckling flew into the butter tub, then into the meat barrel and out again.

Well, what a sight! The woman shrieked and struck at him with the fire tongs. The children laughed and shouted as they tumbled over one another trying to catch him. It was a good thing that the door was open! The duckling flew out among the bushes and newly fallen snow and lay there quite exhausted.

It would be too sad to tell of the loneliness and misery the duckling had to endure that long, hard winter as he lay out in the swamp among the reeds.

Then the sun began to shine again and the larks to sing. Beautiful spring had come. The duckling raised his wings and found that they beat the air fiercely and bore him strongly away. Before he knew just how it happened, he found he was in a large garden. Apple trees stood in blossom, and sweet lilac flowers hung their long green branches down the winding canals. Oh, it was so beautiful and fresh! Then out from the thicket came three lovely white swans. They ruffled their wings and floated ever so lightly over the water. The duckling saw they were the splendid creatures he had seen in the autumn. He felt a sudden sadness.

"I will fly over to those royal birds, and they will beat me because I, who am so ugly, dare to come near them. Still, it is better to be killed by them than to be bitten by the ducks, pecked at by the chickens, kicked by the girl who takes care of the duck yard, and suffer the hardships of winter!"

He flew out into the water and swam toward the beautiful swans. They watched and came sailing over to him, ruffling their wings.

"Kill me!" cried the poor duckling. He bent his head down upon the water and waited for death.

But what was this he saw in the clear water? Below him he saw his own image, but he was no longer a large, clumsy duckling, hideous and ugly. He was himself—a swan! The big swans swam around him and stroked him with their beaks.

Some children came into the garden and pointed to the swans. "Look!" the youngest one cried. "There is a new one!" They clapped their hands and danced around, then ran to get their parents. Bread and cake were thrown into the water, and everyone cried, "The new one is the most beautiful of all, so young and handsome!"

The old swans bowed their heads before him. He felt quite shy and hid his head under his wing, for he did not know what else to do. He was so happy, yet not conceited, because a good heart is never proud. "I never dreamed of so much happiness when I was the ugly duckling!" he said.

He thought of how he had been mocked and kicked about. Now he heard them say he was the loveliest bird of all.

The lilacs bent their branches down in the water before him. The sun shone warm and mild. He fluffed his feathers, lifted his slender neck, and from his heart there came a cry of total joy and contentment.